The MOFFATTS on the Road

Home Is Where the Heart Is

By Nancy Krulik

SCHOLASTIC INC.

New York Toronto London Auckland Sydney
Mexico City New Delhi Hong Kong

ISBN 0-439-13686-5

William Bell & Associates, Inc.
Personal Management — Nashville, TN

12 11 10 9 8 7 6 5 4 3 2 1   0 1 2 3 4 5 6/0

Printed in the U.S.A.
First Scholastic printing, June 2000

For Danny, Amanda, and Ian,
who always know where my heart is.
—NEK

Scott Moffatt pulled out his new Stephen King horror novel, lay down on his bunk, and began to read. Some people might find it really tough to read on a moving bus, but not Scott. He'd spent most of his life traveling on a tour bus. At this point, there wasn't anything he couldn't manage in a moving vehicle.

Ever since Scott and his triplet brothers, Bob, Clint, and Dave, were little boys, they'd been singing together as a group. At first they were just cute little kids, harmonizing country tunes at local clubs in their native Canada. As they began playing their own instruments, their popularity grew. That's when the guys, their dad, and stepmom took to the road on a tour bus, and started playing concerts in the United States, Canada, and abroad. They played gigs in Nashville, Las Vegas, and even the White House!

But it wasn't until the Moffatts grew up and

began writing and recording their own pop tunes that they really joined the big leagues. Now, here it was, twelve years after they'd first started performing professionally, and the guys had their own hit CD on the charts, Chapter 1: A New Beginning. One of their songs, "Until You Loved Me," had even been included on the sound track for a Drew Barrymore movie! Another, "Misery," was chosen for the Teaching Mrs. Tingle movie sound track. The Moffatts' pictures were on the covers of all the teen magazines, their concerts were guaranteed sold-out successes, and everywhere they went, screaming girls were sure to follow.

Life was totally sweet!

Right now, as Scott read his new novel, his brothers were resting quietly on their own bunks — also taking a chance to relax after an extremely hectic morning. The Moffatts had just left New York City, where they'd performed for an extremely enthusiastic audience at TV's Live with Regis and Kathie Lee show. Now they were on their way to a huge, sold-out show scheduled for tomorrow night in Boston.

But the Moffatts had never taken success for granted. After all, it hadn't been so long ago that they were playing clubs in smaller cities.

Scott looked up from his book and glanced out the bus window. He noticed a green traffic sign by the side of the road. It read HOLLINGSDALE, 5 MILES.

"Hey! Check it out," Scott called to his brothers. "We're right near Hollingsdale. You guys remember the time we played there?"

Bob Moffatt reached across the aisle and rubbed the buzz cut on top of his brother Clint's head. "Wasn't that the place where you cut off all your hair?" he reminded him.

Clint laughed and ran his fingers through his super-short, brown and bleached-blond locks. "Best move I ever made."

Scott sighed as the bus rolled past the sign, and continued its way north to Boston.

"I know I'll always remember Hollingsdale," he remarked quietly.

"We all will," Dave agreed. "I mean, how could we ever forget. . . ."

Chapter One

"Hey Scott!" Bob Moffatt cried out. "Heads up!"

A red rubber ball went flying across the Moffatts' tour bus and hit Scott Moffatt right on the side of his head.

"Cut it out, will ya?" Scott warned his younger brother as he rubbed his head where the ball hit. "I'm trying to write a song here."

"Sorry," Bob mumbled. "I thought you'd wanna have a catch." He got up, grabbed the ball, and walked over to the far end of the bus, where his brother, Dave, was listening to music on his Discman.

"What're you listening to?" Bob asked.

Dave didn't answer. He obviously couldn't hear his brother over the music. But instead of tapping Dave on his shoulder to get his attention, Bob shouted out his question a little louder. "I said . . . *what are you listening to?*"

Dave pulled the headphones from his ears. "'Nine Lives,' by Aerosmith."

"Cool," Clint called from his bunk, where he was busy reading a Stephen King thriller. "I love that tune. Turn it up."

"Okay." Dave unplugged the headphones from his Discman, and connected a pair of portable speakers. Within seconds, Steven Tyler's unmistakable vocals filled the bus. It didn't take long for Bob, Clint, and Dave to chime in, singing along with the veteran rock band.

As his brothers provided the harmonies for Steven Tyler, Scott's face reddened with anger. The triplets never seemed to listen to him, even though Scott felt they owed him at least a little respect. After all, at almost seventeen, Scott *was* eleven months older than they were. "Hey you guys, I'm trying to work on a melody line over here. How'm I supposed to do that with you three blasting Aerosmith?"

"We're not blasting it," Dave insisted. "We're just listening to it. Chill out! You've been totally cranky ever since we hit the road this morning. Are you having writer's block or something?"

Scott tucked a lock of his shoulder-length, brown-and-blond-streaked hair behind his ear, and refused to answer. He hated to admit it, but Dave was right. He *was* having a case of writer's block. A bad case, in fact.

Usually, songs just poured out of Scott. He

and his brothers had been able to write some of their best tunes in less than two hours. But today the blank piece of music paper seemed to be staring back at him, mocking him — daring him to write notes on it.

Scott looked over at his brothers. They seemed happy enough. Identical twins Clint and Bob were laughing as they tried to imitate Aerosmith drummer Joey Kramer's rhythm by drumming on their thighs with pencils. As they bopped their heads up and down, their long brown hair seemed to mesh together, as though it were attached to just one head. The third triplet, Dave, was playing a wild air guitar solo. Dave loved to play at being the "punk Moffatt," running his fingers through his short brown hair to spike it up a bit.

The triplets were having a blast. Life on the road wasn't getting to them at all. That was really frustrating for Scott, because life on the road *was* getting to him. Even though the Moffatts traveled on what could only be called the ultimate tour bus — complete with extremely comfortable sleeping bunks, state-of-the-art stereo systems, VCRs, video game consoles (which the boys were usually too busy to use), and Internet-connected computers — *life* on the bus was not all that pleasant. After all, there was only one bus, and there were four Moffatt brothers, not to mention their dad, Frank, their stepmom, Sheila, and the driver on board. Sometimes it felt like

3

the Moffatts were on top of each other 24/7. And like a lot of people, Scott needed his space.

"I'm so sick of this bus!" Scott declared, as he slammed the pad of music paper shut, stood up, and walked over to Clint's bunk. "I never have any privacy. It'd be so awesome to be able to go into my own room and close the door."

"I know what you mean," Clint agreed. "It's great to be out on tour and everything, but it's been so long since we were back home. We just go from one hotel to another. Sometimes I feel like we're homeless or something."

Bob twirled a lock of his long brown hair around his finger. "Speaking of *home*, a home-cooked meal wouldn't be bad once in a while, either."

Just the mention of food made Scott's stomach rumble. Like his brothers, Scott seemed to be hungry all the time. "Hey dad," he called up to the front of the bus. "Didn't I see a sign for a rest stop a few miles back? I'm starved."

The boys' father, Frank Moffatt, laughed. "How unusual," he teased. "Okay, one quick stop for a snack, and then we're on the road again. I want to hit the hotel before dark. You guys have some schoolwork to do before you go to bed. There won't be time to do it tomorrow — we've got a rehearsal, a photo shoot for the Arts and Leisure section of the *Hollingsdale Times*, and an interview at a radio station. That's *really* important because this concert isn't far from

New York City. The radio station is powerful enough to broadcast all the way into the city. And you guys know how big *that* market is."

The guys nodded in agreement. They were excited about the possibility of reaching so many fans. And they weren't surprised that their dad had made sure that they would find time to do their schoolwork. The Moffatts were used to fitting in their education whenever they could. Because they were on the road so much, their father and stepmom had taken on the additional responsibility of home-schooling their sons.

Some people felt bad for the guys when they told them that they were home-schooled. They figured they must miss the social life of going to a regular high school. But the Moffatt brothers didn't see it like that at all. In their eyes, home-schooling was great, because they were able to customize their studies to subjects that interested them. And, unlike kids who were studying geography by looking at the maps that were hung in their classrooms, the Moffatts were actually able to visit countries in Asia and Europe, meet the people there, and eat the native foods. So while most kids were sitting behind desks in classrooms, looking at pictures in textbooks of Shakespeare's home in Stratford-upon-Avon, the Moffatts could be walking through the actual house on one of their days off from touring in England.

Traffic was light, so it only took a few minutes before the bus driver pulled into a rest stop along the New York State Thruway. The boys bounded off the bus and raced into the Taco Bell. There was no time to waste — there were *burritos* waiting inside!

As the guys waited in line and decided on their orders, they noticed two girls sitting alone in a booth. The girls were pointing at the Moffatts, and giggling.

"I think they recognize us," Dave whispered.

"They're really cute," Clint added.

"Why don't we go over and say hi?" Bob suggested.

"We don't really have time to get to know them," Scott said. "We've got to be back on the bus in a couple of minutes."

Dave laughed. "Well, to tell you the truth, big bro, I'd rather spend *my* couple of minutes with some cute girls, than alone at a table with you."

There was no arguing with that kind of logic, so the Moffatts got in line, bought their burritos, and walked over to the girls' table.

"Hi," Dave greeted them without even a touch of shyness. Talking to girls came easily to Dave. He flashed a bright smile and stared at them with his big brown eyes.

The girls giggled again.

"Did you recognize us from a show in your town?" Bob asked them. "Or from a magazine?"

"Well, actually, we were sort of staring because one of you has a long piece of toilet paper stuck to your shoe," one girl explained as she brushed a crumb from her bright yellow sweater. She pointed down at Scott's feet. Scott felt a warm blush of embarrassment cover his cheeks as he kicked the paper from his heel. First he had writer's block and now he looked like a total dork in front of some very pretty girls! What a rotten day this was turning into.

"But, we *did* recognize you guys. And we would *love* an autograph," the second girl admitted shyly as she smiled at Scott and nervously pushed up the sleeves of her red sweatshirt. She obviously felt bad that they embarrassed him — especially since he was so adorable when he blushed. "We just heard 'Misery' on the car radio. It's a great tune."

Scott grinned back at her. "Thanks," he said. "I like that one, too. It's a little different from what we usually play."

"Do you mind if we sit with you two?" Dave asked.

"Not at all." The girl in the yellow sweater flipped her long blond hair over her shoulder, moved over on the bench, and smiled. "My name's Carenna, and this is my sister, Ilana."

"Are you traveling by yourselves?" Bob asked.

"No. But Ilana has her license," she added proudly. "Actually, our parents are over there at the frozen yogurt stand. *We're* more into chips and salsa."

"You're my kind of people." Bob took a bite of an overstuffed taco.

"I'm going for my license soon," Scott told Ilana. "Was the driving test hard?"

Ilana shook her head. "Not really. Just the parallel parking part. But I got my license on the first try!"

"That's cool," Scott congratulated her.

As the guys scarfed down their food and joked with Carenna and Ilana, Scott began to relax. He knew that sooner or later a melody would come to him — or to one of his brothers. Besides, they had enough songs to fill a concert, even without a new song.

All too soon, Frank walked over to the booth where his sons were sitting. "Time to go guys," he told them. "Finish up."

"Will you sign this before you go?" Carenna handed Scott a napkin and a pen that she had pulled from her backpack. "Otherwise no one at home will ever believe we had a snack with the Moffatts."

Scott smiled. He took the pen and wrote, "Carenna and Ilana: It was great meeting you. Salsa and chips rule! Love, Scott Moffatt," on the napkin. Then he passed the paper and pen along to his brothers for their autographs.

After signing the napkin, Scott and the triplets

said good-bye and left the restaurant. They sucked down the last few sips of their sodas as they began walking back toward the parking lot.

"Dave, you're such a flirt," Bob teased as they boarded the tour bus.

"They flirted first. I just returned the favor," he replied. "But I guess we should all thank Scott for getting the girls' attention in the first place!" He pointed down to Scott's feet.

Scott playfully grabbed his brother around the neck and pretended to strangle him. Then he climbed into the bus and crawled back onto his bunk. He pulled out his guitar and began tuning the strings as the bus made its way back onto the highway. As he turned the pegs, Scott hoped that the burrito break was all the rest his mind needed. Maybe *now* he could come up with a great hook for a new song.

But before Scott could even play one chord, an awful odor began filling the tour bus. It seemed to be coming from Bob's bed.

"Whoa! What *is* that smell?" Clint called out. "Bob did you take your shoes off again?"

"Very funny," Bob replied. "I was just about to ask you the exact same thing."

Scott got off his bed and took a peek under Bob's bunk.

"Guys, I think I've found the source of the problem," he announced.

Chapter Two

Scott reached under the bunk, and pulled out a small, frightened dog. The pup, who had been hiding quietly before, now let out a huge, deep bark. Scott had to laugh. It seemed strange for such a small animal to have such a big voice.

The pup continued to bark as the guys all walked closer to take a look at him. He was a really strange-looking animal. His nose was long and snoutlike, which sort of made up for the short stubbiness of his tail. His body was long, with legs low to the ground. His shaggy coat was a combination of colors — he had equal parts of black, brown, tan, and gray fur. Obviously the dog was a mutt, but even the smartest of vets would have had a tough time figuring out what breeds had been combined to create this creature. Sadly, from the look (and the smell) of him, it was obvious that the mongrel hadn't been cared for by anyone for a very long time — if ever.

"Where did that dog come from?" Sheila Moffatt asked as she joined her stepsons in the back of the bus.

"He must've snuck on board while we were in the restaurant," Scott replied. "He doesn't have any tags. I'll bet he's a stray."

Bob nodded in agreement. "He's probably been eating food from the garbage Dumpsters behind the restaurant."

Dave held his nose. "He sure smells that way, anyhow."

"So what are we going to do with him?" Clint asked finally.

Sheila looked into her stepsons' faces. Somehow she had a feeling that the guys were going to want to keep the dog. "Look," she began gently. "Touring is no life for a dog."

"It's better than being all alone," Scott countered.

"I agree," Sheila replied. "But what would *really* be great is if we could find this dog a family that had a nice house, with a really big yard, and a few kids who could play with him and take care of him properly." Sheila watched as the guys' faces fell with disappointment. She shrugged her shoulders. "Dogs need room to run and people who are around a lot of the time to love them. We've always told you that being musicians comes with sacrifices, and this is one of those times. You have to admit, we're not exactly your typical family. If the dog stayed with us, he'd always be cooped up in the bus, spending his days in hotel rooms — that is, if we could even find hotels that allowed dogs."

At first the guys didn't say a word. They knew their stepmom was right.

"How're we going to find him a home?" Clint asked finally.

"When we get to the hotel, we'll look in the yellow pages for a local animal shelter and drop him off. They'll find him a home."

"We'll find a shelter that has a no-destroy policy, right Sheila?" Scott asked nervously as he stared into the dog's big brown eyes. Scott knew that some shelters only kept their dogs for a few months, and then, if no one adopted them and gave them a home, the shelter put the dogs to sleep. But there were other shelters that managed to keep their dogs alive no matter what — and that was the only kind of place he would give the dog to. Obviously this stray had come to the Moffatts for help. Scott felt a great responsibility to make sure that no harm came to him.

"Absolutely," Sheila assured Scott. "I wouldn't have it any other way."

The guys finally agreed to turn their new four-legged friend over to an animal shelter when they reached Hollingsdale. Bob reached over to pet the pup on his head. At first, the animal jumped up with a yelp — the sudden, kind touch from a human hand had frightened him. It was something he had never felt before. But somehow, the little fellow sensed that the Moffatts were no threat to him. He quieted down, and then lay still beneath Bob's hand.

While Bob comforted the pooch, the other Moffatts went around opening up all the windows on the bus. The dog really stunk, but at least the movement of fresh air as the bus rolled along the highway helped to lessen the stench.

For a while all was quiet on the Moffatt tour bus. The mutt was lulled into a resting state by the motion of the bus, and Bob's gentle hand. One by one, the brothers went back to their bunks and began reading and listening to CDs.

But before long, the bus was in a huge patch of heavy traffic and came to a standstill. There was construction ahead, and now the highway was more like a parking lot than a roadway. Without the movement of the wheels beneath him, the stray was no longer calm. He leaped to his feet and began barking nervously.

"What do we do with him now?" Dave asked his brothers.

"Well, they say music soothes the savage beast," Scott suggested.

"I'm with ya," Clint agreed.

Scott pulled out his guitar and began strumming the opening bars to "Misery." The triplets started singing along.

The Moffatts' sweet harmonies filled the bus. It was a beautiful sound, until, unfortunately, the pup felt a sudden need to sing along. He howled louder and louder as the guys belted out an unplugged version of one of their most famous songs. It was almost as though the hound believed that he was part of the group.

"I've got the perfect name for this little guy," Scott laughed as the family finished singing. "We should call him 'Harmony'!"

Because of the heavy traffic, the Moffatts' tour bus didn't roll into the hotel parking lot until after dark. By now the local animal shelters would most certainly be closed.

"So what're we gonna to do with Harmony?" Dave asked.

"I doubt dogs are allowed in this hotel," Frank replied. "But don't worry, he'll be fine in the bus for the night."

"I thought you weren't supposed to leave animals in cars," Scott remarked.

Frank nodded. "That's true. Especially in the heat. But this tour bus is different. It's big and roomy — more like a mobile home. He's got plenty of room to sleep, and tonight the temperature is nice and mild. We'll get him some dog food, and a bowl of water, and leave the windows open for him." He sniffed the air. "Of course, we'll have to disinfect the bus when he leaves!"

As his father and brothers left the dog alone on the bus, Scott looked into Harmony's frightened brown eyes. "Don't worry," he told the pooch. "I'll think of something."

Scott dashed into the hotel lobby and met up with his brothers. The guys sat on the couch as their parents checked the group into the hotel. Scott and the triplets were tired from the long trip. Their clothes were wrinkled (except, of course, for Clint's. Clint was too much of a neat freak to ever get wrinkled. *His* clothes were always perfectly neat and pressed), and they all had a distinctive "doggy" odor about them — thanks to Harmony.

The hotel manager, a small, thin, balding man named Mr. Bratt, looked over at the couch and sighed. "Mr. and Mrs. Moffatt, I want you to know that we don't particularly love having rock and roll bands at the Hollingsdale Plaza Hotel. They are usually nothing but trouble. And, seeing that your sons are still teenagers, well, you can imagine our concern. I hope you know that we will consider you to be financially responsible for any destruction to their room."

Sheila Moffatt took a deep controlling breath.

Then she smiled as sweetly she could. "Mr. Bratt, I assure you that there will be no problems. We're all seasoned travelers, and quite responsible. I'm sure you won't even know we're here."

"Well, I hope not. As it is, we've taken many precautions to keep the press from knowing that the Moffatts are staying at the hotel. We don't want any crowds of screaming girls filling up our lobby and disturbing the other guests."

Sheila nodded. "I think keeping things quiet is a good idea — it's much safer for the guys. That's *our* top priority."

Mr. Bratt scratched at the small black moustache beneath his pointed nose. "Oh, yes, of course," he mumbled, as he handed Frank two sets of room keys. "Your room is across the hall from the boys' suite — it'll be easier for you to keep an eye on them that way."

"Thank you," Frank said as he took the keys. "Come on guys. Let's go up and get settled."

Scott looked back toward the bus. Then he glanced over toward the elevator, where his parents and brothers had already assembled. "I'll be right there, Dad," he called out. "I just need to run out to the bus and grab my guitar. I've got an idea I might want to sketch out."

Frank nodded. "We'll meet you upstairs. Room 1422."

Scott raced outside and hurried onto the bus.

Harmony was so happy to see him that he darted toward the door. Scott reached down to pet him on the head.

"Calm down, boy. You've gotta be really quiet, or we'll never be able to pull this off." Scott picked up the pup, and hid him underneath his jacket. He held Harmony steady with his right hand as he picked up his guitar with his left. Then he hopped off the bus, pushed the door open, and walked back into the lobby.

Mr. Bratt caught a whiff of a strong odor as Scott passed by the front desk and made his way to the elevators. "Teenagers!" the hotel manager exclaimed as the elevator doors closed. "The least they could do is take a shower once in a while!"

Chapter Three

Scott stopped outside room 1422, and listened quietly. He could hear the triplets laughing as they unpacked their clothes inside the suite. They were goofing on Clint, who was apparently refolding each of his sweaters before placing them in his drawer. In the room across the hall, he could hear his father and stepmother talking behind closed doors about the arrogance of Mr. Bratt.

Scott was happy Frank and Sheila were already settling into their room. That meant that he could go into the guys' suite without Harmony being discovered. Scott knew his brothers would do whatever was necessary to keep Harmony's presence in the hotel a secret. He also knew his dad would definitely make him put the dog back on the bus.

Scott knocked on the door. Bob opened it, and let his older brother in. As Scott walked by, Bob held his nose. "Yuck! You really smell like Harmony," he declared. "Were you rolling in the Dumpsters, too?"

Scott shot his brother an annoyed look. Then he carefully opened his jacket to reveal the hidden pooch, who was huddled against Scott's chest. "Shhh," Scott warned the hound — and his brothers. "We have to keep this a secret."

Clint smiled. "Then we'd better give him a good bath. It'll be hard to keep him hidden if he stinks like that."

"I'm already on it!" Dave announced as he went into the bathroom and began to fill the tub.

Harmony would not go willingly into the water. As soon as Scott carried him into the bathroom, the crazed canine dove from his arms, and ran back out into the bedroom. Worried that the dog might bark and alert his parents, Scott turned on the TV — not so loudly that the sound would upset any of the hotel's other guests, but at a volume that at least would mask any barks Harmony let out.

It took all four brothers to get Harmony smelling sweet. Bob and Dave actually had to get in the tub and hold the mutt still, while Scott washed his head and ears, and Clint worked on his legs and paws.

Finally, Harmony was clean. The boys helped the small pup out of the tub, and dried him with a soft white towel. Then Scott took him into the bedroom he was sharing with Dave and shut the door.

"I'll call room service and order up a hamburger for Harmony," Dave told the others.

"Order some for us, too," Clint suggested. "Make mine with a side of fries."

"Coming right up," Dave assured him.

"While we wait for the food, we'd better get going on that algebra that dad left for us," Scott warned his younger brothers. "We promised we'd have it done by the time we went to bed. And we don't want to give Dad and Sheila any reasons to be suspicious."

The guys got right to work. When the food arrived, they fed Harmony in the bedroom and munched on their snacks while they figured out the algebra equations.

Clint was first to finish the homework. He snuck quietly into the bathroom as his brothers worked out their math problems. The others were so intent on what they were doing, they never even noticed he'd left the room.

Suddenly, Bob heard a loud click as the hotel door opened. He looked up and let out a small shout of surprise. Standing in the doorway were two girls he'd never seen before. The girls didn't say a word. They just stood there, staring at the boys.

"Can I help you?" Bob asked.

"We, um, I . . ." the smaller of the two girls stammered.

"I told you they'd be here," her companion whispered.

"How'd you open the door? Clint asked them. "I thought we had the only keys."

"You left the door unlocked," the taller of the girls explained. "I just turned the knob. But I didn't mean to frighten you guys or anything. We just really wanted to meet you, and so, we y'know, kind of followed . . ."

"Why don't you come in and sit down for a minute?" Dave interrupted. He motioned for the girls to come into the suite. "You look a little shocked."

The girls sat down and stared at Scott, Dave, and Bob. "I-I-I can't believe it," the smaller girl declared. "Is it really you?"

Scott laughed. "It's really us. Who are you?"

"I'm Justine," the taller of the two girls told him.

"And I'm, um, um . . ." The smaller girl blushed. She was so flustered she couldn't remember her own name.

"She's Lyndsey," Justine told them. "She's just a little freaked out at seeing you up close. We've never done anything like this before. Honest."

"I believe you," Scott assured them. "But it's cool. How did you know we were here?"

"We saw your tour bus drive into town, and we kind of followed you here on our bikes," Justine explained. She wiped a strand of her long, curly brown hair from her face. "We're, like, your biggest fans. So when we heard you were coming to town, we kept an eye out for the bus."

"Okay, so that explains how you got to the hotel. But how did you find out what room we were in? Did that hotel manager tell you?" Bob asked.

Justine shook her head. "Are you kidding? That guy never even bothers with kids. He hates us. You'd think he'd never been one! Actually, we walked into the hotel lobby right after you did, and hid over by the telephones. We heard your dad tell Scott which room to go to." She looked at the three brothers. "Where's Clint?" she asked finally.

The bathroom door opened. "Did someone call my name?"

There was a collective gasp. Everyone stared at Clint in disbelief. He had gone into the bathroom and completely cut off his long brown hair. He'd even gone so far as to use a razor to give himself a buzz cut.

"What'd you do?" Bob exclaimed.

"What's it look like? I cut my hair."

"Why?"

Clint sat down next to his identical twin and smiled. "Because I'm tired of being mistaken for you. Not that you're not a great-looking guy or anything."

Bob laughed. "Which, as my identical twin, makes you a great-looking guy, too, right?"

"Naturally." Clint turned to Justine and Lyndsey. "So what do you girls think?"

"I love it," Lyndsey declared.

"I like it," Justine agreed. "But I think it could be even cooler."

"How?" Clint asked.

"Well, do you have any hair bleach?"

The triplets all pointed to Scott. "He does," they said all at once.

Scott nodded and twisted a light-brown strand of hair around his finger and blushed slightly. "I bleach a few highlights once in a while," he admitted. "Do you want to use it?"

Justine nodded. Scott found his travel bag, and pulled out a small bottle of hair bleach. He handed it over.

"Come with me," Justine told Clint. She led him into the bathroom, and closed the door. A little while later, the two emerged. The hair in the front of Clint's head was yellow-blond, while the rest of his hair remained dark-brown.

"So, what do you think?" Clint asked Lyndsey and his brothers.

"Awesome!" Lyndsey shouted excitedly.

"That's all I needed to hear," Clint thanked her.

Scott stood up. "I hate to be a total party pooper, but we've got to get to sleep. We've got a big interview tomorrow, and a photo shoot, too."

Justine and Lyndsey stood up and got ready to leave. Justine stopped and turned to Clint. "Do you think I could have a lock of your hair?" she asked him.

"Anything for my new favorite hairstylist," he answered her with a wink. He went into the bathroom and returned with a lock of long brown hair for each of the girls.

"Thanks!" Lyndsey exclaimed.

"I'll never forget this," Justine promised.

As the guys got ready for bed, Justine and Lyndsey sat in the lobby of the Hollingsdale Plaza hotel, staring at the locks of Clint's hair.

"I'm going to put this in a locket and wear it around my neck forever!" Justine exclaimed.

"I can't believe I'm holding Clint's hair in my hand," Lyndsey added. "This is priceless! Better than any other Moffatts souvenir I have. We're so lucky that we got there just after he cut his hair!"

"You should've seen the bathroom. He had a whole trash can full of that beautiful brown hair. I could've taken the whole thing home with me." Justine squealed. "The kids at school are going to be soooo jealous! We are the luckiest girls in the entire world!"

A smile broke out on Mr. Bratt's face as he eavesdropped on the girls' conversations. "Maybe those teenagers will do me some good after all," he muttered quietly to himself.

Chapter Four

"Okay, smile!" The photographer for the *Hollingsdale Times* clicked his camera as the guys put their arms around one another, and flashed giant smiles in his direction.

"Great!" the photographer exclaimed. "Now, let's have one of each of you alone. Scott, how about you go first?"

Scott picked up his guitar and walked over to a stool that had been placed in the center of the room. He faced the camera and looked brooding and pensive. The photographer adjusted the lighting, and snapped pictures from different angles.

"Nice," the photographer complimented him. "Very artistic. Now, how about taking another one, but with a smile this time? And would you mind pretending to read the paper?"

The photographer's assistant handed Scott a copy of the *Hollingsdale Times*. Scott knew exactly how this photo should look. He'd done the same thing lots of times for fan magazines. He held the newspaper so that everyone could see its name. Then he grinned, and managed to look at both the newspaper and the camera at the same time. It was a trick he'd developed over the years.

As soon as the photographer was finished with Scott, it was Clint's turn to have his picture taken. Like his brothers, Clint was very comfortable in front of the camera. After all, the boys had been performing for most of their lives (starting when they were just little guys dressed in matching outfits!), and photo shoots were part of the business. But today, Clint was especially up and excited. After all, this was the first time his new buzz cut would be seen by the public! Clint thought that his new 'do was really awesome. Hey, even his *brothers* had complimented him on it, and they were not famous for giving props to one another. Sheila had commented that the haircut made him appear older and more sophisticated — exactly the look Clint was hoping for. Even their dad — who was definitely shocked when he saw his son come down to breakfast with practically a shaved head and blond bangs — had to admit that the look was totally Clint, and really great!

With that kind of encouragement, Clint couldn't wait to see how his new hair would look in photographs. In fact, he balked when the photographer asked him to wear a New York Yankees batting helmet for one of the photos, because that would cover his head. Instead, he volunteered to pose for the camera in a Mets baseball jersey that one of the sportswriters had in a desk drawer.

The photo shoot went very smoothly; the whole thing was over in less than two and a half hours. As the guys left the offices of the *Hollingsdale Times*, they were in excellent moods. The Moffatts weren't scheduled to rehearse until late afternoon, and their radio interview wouldn't be until 9:00 that night — the perfect time because many of their fans would be tuning in after doing their homework. That meant the rest of the morning was free. The boys could do whatever they wanted!

"Well, I'm off to the mall," Bob announced.

"Me, too," Dave agreed. "I definitely need some new T-shirts."

"Maybe you'll keep your grubby paws off mine then," Clint laughed. "I'm coming, too. How 'bout you Scott? You up for a trip to the mall?"

Scott shook his head. "No thanks. I need to work on that new song. I'm heading back to the hotel."

"Wait a minute. Nobody's leaving here until I find out what's going on with that dog," Frank

28

interrupted his sons. "Has anyone walked him today? Or fed him? Or given him fresh water?"

Bob nodded. "Of course we have, Dad. We ordered him a hamburger. Harmony's fine. Great. He seems really happy."

Frank smiled. "I know what you're thinking, but there's no way you're keeping that dog. You promised to look into shelters. And if you won't do it, I will."

"We'll do it, Dad, we promise. But we still have a few days here, right?" Scott replied.

Frank nodded. "Yes. But he's not coming with us to the next stop on the tour, okay?"

The guys all nodded in agreement.

"Okay, you guys go on to the mall. Sheila and I are going to have some lunch at the café. We'll meet at the arena for a rehearsal at four o'clock."

The triplets took off for the mall, and Scott went back to the hotel to work.

As soon as Scott opened the door to the suite, Harmony ran up to greet him.

"Boy, you must've been lonely here," Scott told the dog as he stooped down to pet him on the head. "I'm going to play the guitar now, okay?"

Harmony had no idea what Scott was saying, but he was happy to hear his voice. So the pooch stayed close to Scott's heels as he walked around the room, gathering his pencils and paper and tuning his guitar. When Scott sat on the couch, the dog plopped down by his feet and waited for Scott to play. Scott laughed. "You want to hear a song, Harmony?" Scott asked the wide-eyed pup. "Okay, here's one." Scott absentmindedly strummed an old three-bar blues tune, just to get himself warmed up. Unfortunately, Harmony tried to bark along with the music. Scott groaned. If the dog kept this up, they'd surely be found out.

"If you don't stop howling, you're going to have to go back to the bus. You've got to be quiet," Scott told his canine companion. Then he began to strum the strings of his guitar. And once again, Harmony barked along.

"This isn't going to work," Scott shook his head, and began packing his pad and pencils into his backpack. "I can't write with you barking. I'm going to go somewhere more quiet. I'll see you later. Be good."

As Scott closed the door to the suite, he placed the DO NOT DISTURB sign around the knob. He didn't want the housekeeping staff to wander in and discover Harmony.

A few moments later, as Scott walked out through the hotel lobby, he made sure to give Mr. Bratt a hearty wave. Scott knew exactly how the hotel manager felt about having the

Moffatts as guests, and he couldn't resist getting under his skin just a little bit.

But to Scott's surprise, the manager smiled and waved back at him. "Good morning, Mr. Moffatt," he greeted Scott. "I trust you had a nice evening. Have a lovely day."

Scott was definitely caught off guard by that friendly greeting. "Um, thanks," he murmured. "You, too."

As he walked out the door, Scott couldn't help wondering, *What was that all about?*

Chapter Five

The Hollingsdale Plaza Hotel was located right in the middle of town. That meant that Scott could walk just about anywhere he wanted to. Scott remembered seeing a coffee shop at the end of the block. That seemed as good a place as any to plant himself. He decided to stop in and have a snack.

A set of bells that were attached to the door rang out as Scott entered the coffee shop. Scott flinched. He didn't really want to have any attention drawn to himself this morning. He just wanted to work. Luckily, the coffee shop was nearly empty when Scott walked in. The breakfast crowd had already gone on to work, and the lunch group wasn't due for another hour or two. Only a few regulars were there, and they were all seated at the counter, having a heated debate over which channel to watch on the TV that was mounted above the counter.

Scott found himself a quiet booth in the back of the coffee shop, and sat down. A waitress came over a few minutes later.

"What'll you have, son?" she asked him.

"Just a hot chocolate," Scott told her.

"Coming right up," the waitress assured him. She walked away and gave the order to the cook who stood behind the counter.

While he waited for his hot chocolate, Scott opened his backpack and took out his pad and pencils. He tapped out a beat on the table, and wracked his brains trying to come up with a new song.

The sound of bells filled the coffee shop again as a new patron opened the door and walked inside. Scott looked up to see a teenage girl wander over toward the counter. She was only about sixteen years old, but her frowning face, slumped shoulders, and tired green eyes made her appear much older. She wore old, worn-out jeans and a big, faded denim jacket that hung loose on her thin body. Her long blond hair looked knotted and scraggly. It seemed to Scott that she must have seen a lot in her short life. He couldn't help but think that this girl looked as sad as anyone he had ever seen.

"A large cup of coffee please." The girl reached into her pocket and pulled out some change. She plunked two quarters down on the counter and smiled at the waitress. "To go," she added.

The waitress took the coins, filled a big Styrofoam cup with coffee, and handed it to the girl. "Careful now, honey," the waitress warned with a kind smile. "It's hot."

The girl sat down at a booth. Scott watched as she added a little milk and three huge, heaping spoonfuls of sugar to the coffee and drank it down quickly. Then the girl picked up the creamer again, and filled the empty cup with milk. She reached behind her to the next booth, and grabbed that creamer, too. She emptied the second creamer into her cup, covered the cup with a plastic lid, stood up, and walked toward the bathroom.

For some reason, the girl's actions totally fascinated Scott. He was no longer worrying about his music. All he could think about was that girl. Who was she? And why was she so sad?

As he waited for the girl to come out of the bathroom, Scott sipped his hot chocolate and scribbled the words, "Sad, Silent Stranger" on his notepad. Finally, he had some inspiration. It wasn't a melody, but having a title was a start.

When the girl finally came out of the bathroom, her face was scrubbed clean, and her hair was tied back neatly in a ponytail. She gripped her Styrofoam cup tightly in her hand as she walked toward the door.

Scott couldn't contain his curiosity. This girl

was definitely someone with a secret — and he just had to know what it was. Quickly, he reached into his pocket, pulled out the money for the hot chocolate, added a little extra for a tip, and placed it on the table. He grabbed his notepad and his backpack, and followed the girl out the door.

Hollingsdale wasn't a huge metropolis, but it wasn't a tiny town, either. There were plenty of people walking the streets as Scott tried to follow the girl from the coffee shop. It wasn't easy for him to keep his eye on her. He had to keep in step with the girl while dodging in and out between businesspeople with briefcases and cell phones, mothers wheeling babies in strollers, in-line skaters, and older people who were walking slowly as they did their errands.

He also had to be sure to keep his distance from the girl. Scott didn't want to get too close. He didn't want her to be scared off, thinking some kind of stalker was after her.

The girl turned the corner onto a small side street. Scott followed her as far as the corner, but stopped short of trailing her down the street. Instead, he waited at the corner to see what she would do next.

The tired-looking teen continued walking about halfway down the block. Finally, she came to an old red van that was parked in front of a store that sold antiques and used books. Scott watched as the girl rapped on the window of the van.

A little boy, who looked to be about ten years old, opened the side door and stepped out of the van. Like the girl, he had blond hair, although his was cropped short. He, too, wore old, worn clothing that didn't quite fit correctly. His shirtsleeves were too small, and his pants were far too baggy. The resemblance between the pair was striking: Scott figured they had to be brother and sister.

The girl handed her younger brother the cup of milk. Scott watched as he drank it down thirstily. Then the boy turned and whispered something to his sister. She nodded, and gave him a hug.

The girl and her brother seemed to be involved in a pretty intense conversation. They were too engrossed to notice anyone casually walking by, so Scott made his way down the block and pretended to stop to look in the window of the antique store. What he was *really* looking at was a reflection of the van in the shop window. Through it, Scott could see bags of what appeared to be clothing, an old radio, some broken toys, a few blankets, and four small pillows.

Suddenly, Scott got a sick feeling in the pit of his stomach. Were the girl and her brother *living* in the van?

Chapter Six

While Scott was busy investigating the intriguing girl he'd run into at the coffee shop, the triplets were spending every penny of their allowance money on clothing.

When they'd first arrived at the Hollingsdale Mall, Clint, Bob, and Dave had attempted to shop together. But that was one big disaster. The mall was huge — three stories high. There were all sorts of cool stores. Dave had spotted a sporting goods shop, and wanted to check out some new sweats, which were his favorite kind of clothing. Dave's motto always seemed to be "Comfort first!" Clint, however, was a more stylish dresser. He wanted to head into some boutiques that sold suits — preferably in funny colors like yellow and lime-green. Bob wasn't into sweats or suits. He was more into the surfer look, and was trying to track down some trendy Hawaiian shirts. With the triplets all having such different tastes in clothing, there was no way they could reach a compromise. So, they decided to split up and meet back at the food court in an hour.

Clint spotted the kind of store he was looking for at the far end of the mall's lower level. He was walking in that direction, when he heard a girl calling out his name.

"Oh, my gosh! You're Clint Moffatt!" a small, brown-eyed girl in braids called out as she ran toward him. "I can't believe it's really you. I almost didn't recognize you, until I remembered you'd cut your hair."

Clint ran his fingers through his prickly buzz cut and looked curiously at the girl. That was strange. The pictures of his new buzz wouldn't appear in the *Hollingsdale Times* until Sunday. And nobody but the newspaper photographer, Justine, Lyndsey, and the Moffatt family knew about his new look.

"How'd you know I cut my hair?" he asked, trying not to sound too suspicious.

"The man who sold me this locket told me all about it." She held up a small, metallic, heart-shaped locket that hung from a chain around her neck. She popped open the locket to reveal a few strands of dark brown hair lying neatly inside. "I was so curious about your new hairdo. I think you look really cool like this."

"Thanks," Clint said with a relieved smile. He

had been kind of worried about how the fans would react to his new look. "But what does your locket have to do with my hair?"

The girl laughed. "I read in a magazine that you like to joke around a lot. I guess the fan magazines really do tell the truth. You know what this is. It's a lock of your hair."

"Really?"

"Of course. Everyone's wearing one. The man who was selling them was completely sold out by eleven o'clock this morning. He told me he'd have more soon though."

Clint looked confused. "He did?"

The fan looked at Clint strangely. "Sure he did. Don't you guys have any idea of what Moffatts merchandise is being sold?"

"Of course we do. But . . ."

"Listen, I gotta run. My mom's waiting to pick me up at the entrance," the girl interrupted. "Can I have your autograph?"

Clint nodded, and the girl pulled out a pen and a pad from her fanny pack. As he signed his name, Clint decided that he just didn't have the heart to tell the girl that she had wasted her money on fake Moffatts merchandise.

Clint was sure that the hair in the locket couldn't be his — even though it really looked like it — because each of the brothers were in charge of a specific aspect of the group's career. Nothing they sang, recorded, or sold, went through without at least one of the brothers okaying the deal. Scott's job was overseeing the songwriting and production of the albums. Clint dealt with the road crew. Bob focused on publishing and record sales. Merchandising and licensing was Dave's domain. That meant Dave had to work out deals with clothing companies, stationery manufacturers, and even jewelry makers who wanted to make and sell products that bore the Moffatts' name and likenesses. Clint was pretty sure Dave hadn't okayed the official packaging and selling of Clint Moffatt's hair!

So Clint wondered who was cheating his fans. And that's just what he planned to ask his brothers as soon as he met up with them at the food court.

It wasn't hard for Clint to figure out which table Bob and Dave were sitting at. A crowd of girls had gathered around them. The guys were busy signing autographs as Clint wandered over. He pulled out a pen, and signed a few napkins, address books, and T-shirts himself.

When the group of girls had moved on, Clint sat down and gave his brothers the 411 on what had happened when he'd met the girl with the locket.

"You think maybe it really *is* your hair?" Dave asked.

"Where would someone get it?"

"You gave a bunch of it to Lyndsey and Justine, remember?" Bob suggested as he took a big bite of his hero sandwich. "You said the girl already knew you'd changed your 'do. And Justine and Lyndsey were the only ones besides us who knew about your haircut. Maybe they're . . . uh . . . selling the hair you gave them last night."

"I don't think so," Clint disagreed. "Those girls seemed really sweet. Besides, the photographer knew about it, too."

"But you *did* give them some of your hair," Bob reminded Clint. "That makes them our prime suspects."

Clint nodded. "I guess. But they didn't have enough to sell to a whole lot of people. Besides, this girl told me that she had bought the locket from a man, and that the man was going to have more hair to sell."

Dave shoved two French fries in his mouth and shrugged. "It's a mystery, that's for sure," he admitted. "But there's nothing we can do about it now. We have to get to rehearsal."

Chapter Seven

Scott was already at the G-Clef Music Arena when the triplets arrived. He was standing in the middle of the large outdoor stage, tuning his guitar, and quietly humming the words to "Misery."

"Hey Scott!" Clint called to the stage. But Scott didn't answer. His mind was definitely somewhere else.

"Hello, Captain Daydream! Anybody home?" Dave joked, as he walked over to Scott and playfully waved his hand in front of his big brother's face.

Scott blinked. "Sorry," he apologized. "I just have something on my mind."

"Anything I can help with?" Dave asked sincerely.

For a second, Scott considered telling his brothers about the girl in the coffee shop, but decided to wait until he could figure out what was really going on with her.

"No," Scott said. "But thanks. Anyhow, we should start rehearsing. I was thinking of opening the set with 'Until You Loved Me,' and then moving on to 'Crazy.' We could do 'Written All Over My Heart' after that."

Clint stood and grabbed his bass. "Okay, but 'Written All Over My Heart' could use a little work. Our harmonies were off last time, and the chord changes are a little tricky for me. Do you guys mind if we start the rehearsal with that one?"

Bob took his place at the drums, and Dave stood behind the keyboard and played the opening notes to the song.

As the brothers began singing, Scott relaxed. He was totally caught up in the music. He wasn't thinking about anything except the flow of the notes, and the melding of voices that can only come when the singers are part of the same family.

When the song ended, the guys heard the sweet sound of applause coming from the front row.

"That was killer," Frank Moffatt complimented his sons as he walked up to the stage. "I'm impressed that you guys were here before Sheila and me, and that you got started without us."

Scott choked back a laugh. He realized it was sometimes hard for parents to remember that their kids were almost grown up. Adults always seemed so surprised when teens acted maturely.

For the next three hours, The Moffatts rehearsed songs from their album *Chapter 1: A New Beginning*, as well as a few tunes by other artists, like Lynyrd Skynyrd's "Sweet Home Alabama," and Collective Souls' "Shine." By the time they were finished, they felt confident that they had enough good music to fill the entire show.

"I still wish I had one new tune to surprise the audience with," Scott mused. "I'm working on it. Unfortunately, I've only gotten as far as the title."

"Don't worry," Bob assured him. "We've got plenty of songs. Just let it flow when it's ready."

After the rehearsal, the guys headed right over to WKHO's radio studios. They sat down, met the evening DJs, and slipped on their headphones. As soon as the Moffatts were introduced, the telephones lit up with incoming calls. The guys had a lot of fans in the New York area, and it seemed they all wanted to speak to them.

The radio interview at WKHO was only supposed to last about a half an hour. But there were so many calls coming in to the station, the DJ just trashed his Top 40 music format, and let the brothers answer questions from the fans for his entire shift.

It was exhausting, but it was also fun. The guys really loved the opportunity to connect so personally with their fans. Still, by the time they returned to the hotel, they were talked out and really tired.

But Harmony had no idea that the boys had had such a busy day. He just knew he'd been waiting to see them again. As soon as the Moffatts opened the door to their suite, the pup came bounding out into the hall, jumping and barking excitedly.

"I thought that dog was in the bus," Frank said sternly to his sons.

Busted!

The guys stood quietly and looked at the ground.

"It was my fault, Dad," Scott admitted finally. "Harmony seemed so lonely there. And I was worried that someone would hurt him or something. So, I brought him here. He hasn't been any bother to anyone."

Frank sighed. "A dog doesn't belong in a hotel suite all day. He needs to find a real home. That's why I wanted you boys to call the shelters as soon as we got here."

The guys looked at Harmony. Bob reached down to get him. "I know you're right, Dad," he conceded. "It's just that he's so sweet. We know we've gotta give him up, eventually. But we've never had a pet. And for now, he's ours —

even if it's just for a little while. Besides, no one ever actually told us dogs weren't allowed in the hotel. We all just assumed it."

Sheila looked at her stepsons' faces and tapped Frank gently on the arm. Frank looked in her eyes, and then nodded. "Okay, you win, boys. He can stay in your suite . . . for now. But the first complaint we get, he's at the pound! And, remember, you still have to give him away when we leave Hollingsdale."

Thanking their parents, they scooped up Harmony and carried him back into the suite.

Chapter Eight

Scott woke up early the next morning. He had a lot on his mind. He just *had* to find the girl from the coffee shop. He dressed quietly, and snuck out of the hotel suite before any of his brothers could wake up and ask him questions.

Scott walked past the coffee shop and peeked in the window. There were a lot of customers there — mostly people getting take-out orders to take to their offices. But the girl wasn't there. So Scott decided to go to the only other place he'd seen her — outside the antique store. He hoped the red van was still parked outside the shop.

Sure enough, as soon as Scott turned the corner, he spotted the van. It was parked exactly where he'd last seen it. Scott wanted to go up to the van and peer into the windows to see if anyone was inside, but he was afraid he might frighten the girl if she were there. He decided it would be better to wait a few feet away, and see if anyone came near the van.

For a long time, Scott was alone on the street. Now and then, a passerby would hurry past on the way to work. No one seemed to notice the sixteen-year-old boy who was standing on the corner, or the red van that had been parked on the street for at least two days.

Scott was about to give up and go back to the hotel when suddenly the door to the van opened. Scott held his breath, waiting to see who would come out. Would it be the girl, her brother, or someone else?

Sure enough, it was her — the girl Scott had spotted at the coffee shop the day before. She was huddled up inside the same oversize denim jacket, but this time she was wearing a red sweater underneath and a pair of black leggings. Her long hair was parted on the side, and pulled back by a small brown clip. Scott couldn't help but think that although she was disheveled, she was awfully pretty.

Scott stood silently as the girl walked past. She didn't seem to notice him. Scott let her turn the corner — then he started to follow her.

At first, the girl seemed unaware that anyone was behind her. But then, without warning, she picked up her pace. Scott hurried to keep up. He didn't want to lose her again. But the faster Scott walked, the faster she walked, too.

While she may have started out heading for the coffee shop, the girl suddenly shifted direction, and began walking through a crowded thoroughfare just as the light was changing. She walked across the street, leaving Scott far behind, blocked by the moving traffic.

As the object of his fascination disappeared from sight, Scott's shoulders slumped with frustration. He couldn't say why really, but by now, he'd developed a personal interest in this total stranger. He was certain that she must be living in the van, probably with her brother. But there were so many questions he wanted to ask her. Did she have any parents? Where was she from? Was there anything he could do to help her?

But the girl was gone. And there was nothing for Scott to do now but head back to the hotel. He turned and walked down the street.

On his way, Scott passed the coffee shop. By now, he was very hungry, and the smell of bacon and eggs wafting out to the street from the restaurant was too appealing to resist. Besides, he wanted to pick up a burger to take back to Harmony in a doggie bag. So Scott went inside, and slid into a booth. He opened a menu and waited for the waitress to come to his table. But just then, someone else slid into the seat across from him. Taken by surprise, Scott jumped.

"Okay, so are you going to tell me just why

you're following me?" It was her — the girl! And she was angry.

At first, Scott couldn't speak. He was so happy to finally have the chance to see her up close. He was also embarrassed. After all, he'd just been caught following a total stranger all over town.

"I . . . well . . . uh . . . it's nice to meet you," he stammered, not quite knowing what to say. "I'm Scott Moffatt."

The girl did not reply. She just glared at Scott.

"I saw you in here yesterday," Scott tried to explain lamely.

"So?" the girl huffed. "I go in and out of a lot of places. Just because you saw me in here doesn't give you permission to follow me all around the town. What do you want?"

"I just wanted to get to know you, I guess," Scott admitted.

"Why?"

"I don't know. Something about you I liked, I guess."

The girl softened and shrugged her shoulders. "You could have just introduced yourself," she told Scott. "I don't like people following me."

Scott nodded. "You're right. I wouldn't like that, either. So, let's start over." He held out his hand. "I'm Scott Moffatt. And you are . . . ?"

"Carrie. Carrie Parker." Carrie tentatively

reached out and shook Scott's hand. "Do you live around here?"

Scott shook his head. "Just passing through. My brothers and I are performing Wednesday night at the G-Clef Music Arena."

"Oh, you're a musician?"

"Yes, I play with my brothers. We're in a group called the Moffatts. We've played on a few TV shows, and we've got a few singles out. Maybe you've heard of us?"

"I don't have a TV or a stereo," Carrie explained shyly. "And our radio doesn't work too well. Bad reception I guess. All we can get is a talk station."

"Oh," Scott replied. "Well, maybe you can come to the show on Wednesday and hear us live. That's the way we sound best, anyway. You could be my guest."

"I'm not sure where we'll be on Wednesday," Carrie said sadly. "But I would've liked that. You see, my family's just kind of passing through Hollingsdale, too."

"What'll you two kids have?" The waitress walked over to the booth and interrupted Scott and Carrie's conversation.

"I'll have the bacon and eggs, and an orange juice," Scott ordered. "And pack me up a burger to go. How about you, Carrie?"

"I'll just have a large coffee, also to go," Carrie added. "I need to get back."

"Oh, come on," Scott urged. "Go for the French toast or pancakes or something. It's on me. Think of it as a peace offering. I feel kind of bad about scaring you by following you all over the place this morning. I can understand why it might have made you nervous."

"Well, as long as you put it that way," Carrie accepted with a laugh. "French toast it is."

"And she'll have a large milk, *to go*," Scott told the waitress.

As the woman walked away, Carrie smiled at Scott. "You don't miss a thing, do you?"

Scott grinned. "I did find your actions yesterday kind of intriguing. In fact, I find *you* intriguing. So, tell me everything. Where are you from?"

"You mean now, or originally?"

"Either."

"Well, we used to live in Brooklyn, New York. You can probably hear that in my accent. My dad worked in a factory where they made staplers, staples, and other office supplies. But the company started making their products overseas and the Brooklyn factory closed down. So Dad was out of work. We tried staying in Brooklyn for a while, but there really weren't any factory jobs there. So Dad figured we'd have to move on. Now we're kind of traveling around, while Dad looks for work."

Scott paused. He had to know the truth. Should he just come right out and ask her?

"Is that why you're living in the van?" Scott blurted out finally.

Carrie blushed and didn't answer. She was obviously embarrassed. "Look, I gotta go," she declared finally, as she stood up from the table.

"Hey, it's okay," Scott assured her. "Hard times can fall on anyone's family."

Carrie sat down quietly and sighed. "We lost our apartment in Brooklyn when we couldn't pay the rent," she explained in a whisper. "We tried staying in a homeless shelter for awhile, but it was really awful. I was scared. People stole from other people, and there was so much noise at night. My brother had nightmares all the time. And he was the lucky one. I just didn't go to sleep at all. Finally, my parents figured the shelters were no place for us. Dad sold everything we had left, including his father's pocket watch. He got enough cash to buy the old used van. We travel all over in it, while Dad looks for work. It's pretty close quarters, but at least we're all together, and we're not in those horrible shelters anymore."

"Has your dad had any luck finding work?"

Carrie shook her head. "Not really. Sometimes he'll find work as a day laborer somewhere — he's really good with his hands, and he can fix anything. But that kind of job never lasts, and it doesn't pay much. Dad's looking for something with a steady paycheck so we can settle down somewhere. It's not his fault that he hasn't found a job," she assured Scott. "He'll work at anything. It's just that it's really difficult to get someone to hire you when you have to go to the job interview in old clothes and you have no permanent address to put on the application. But Dad keeps trying. And when he doesn't have an interview he spends all day gathering up old soda cans and bottles. We can trade them in for money. Sometimes I even help him — when I'm not studying."

"Studying?"

Carrie nodded. "Until we move somewhere for good, my mom tutors my brother, Tom, and me. She wants to make sure we don't fall too far behind in our schoolwork."

Scott sat back in his seat, and stared into Carrie's tired, sad eyes. In one way, it was amazing just how much he and Carrie had in common. They both traveled around. They were both home-schooled. And they were both really close to their families. But there was obviously a *huge* difference. The Moffatts traveled the country because they wanted to — in very luxurious style. Scott felt a twinge of guilt as he thought about how much he complained about life on the family bus. He knew he would never joke with his brothers about being "homeless" again.

The waitress came by carrying a tray. She placed Scott's eggs in front of him, and gave Carrie her French toast. Scott watched as Carrie took a bite of the French toast. He could tell she was really enjoying it. Scott figured that she probably didn't have French toast too often. Carrie's family was more likely to eat at soup kitchens, churches, and shelters than in restaurants.

"So that's *my* story," Carrie finished, as she swallowed a syrup-soaked piece of French toast. "Tell me about you. I'm really sorry I'm not caught up in the pop music scene. I'll bet you and your brothers sound great."

Scott smiled. "Well, we think we do, anyway. Maybe someday, when you and your family are settled and having better times, we'll come play in your new hometown. You'll be able to judge for yourself," he said. "My brothers and I have been singing practically since we were babies in Canada. We have this group, and now we're touring to promote our album. We just got back from Asia — a lot more people know about us there that they do here right now, but we're working on changing that."

"What instrument do you play?"

"I'm the guitarist," Scott told her. "And I write a lot of our songs."

"That's so awesome!" Carrie exclaimed. "I've always been amazed by people who can write. Where do you get the inspiration for your music?"

Scott looked at the beautiful, sweet, sad girl across the booth. He thought about the song title he'd scribbled in his notebook the day before. He'd have to change the title now. Carrie wasn't a stranger anymore.

"I get my inspiration from a lot of places," he told her simply. Then he glanced down at his watch with alarm. "Oh, no! I'm late for rehearsal!"

"Are you going to be in trouble?" Carrie asked him.

"Not really. But my brothers will be glad to get on my case for it. Listen, you're not leaving today are you?"

"No. I think Dad has one more interview tomorrow. We'll probably stay around for that."

"Good," Scott said. "You want to have lunch tomorrow, then? I'm a much better conversationalist later in the day."

Carrie laughed. "I think you did pretty well — for someone who's not a morning person. But lunch sounds great."

The waitress brought Carrie her milk in a take-out container, and handed Scott a hamburger to go and the bill.

"Boy, you sure are hungry," Carrie remarked, pointing to the burger.

"Oh, this isn't for me," Scott replied. "It's for my . . ." Scott stopped himself. Maybe it was better not to mention that he and his brothers were hiding a dog in the hotel suite. You never knew who might be listening. "It's for my brother," he lied, finally.

Scott left the money for the meal as well as a tip for the waitress on the table. Then he and Carrie walked out the door.

"I'll meet you here at noon," Scott promised.

Carrie nodded shyly. "Thanks for everything," she told him. "It's been a while since I've had a new friend."

As Carrie walked away down the street, Scott felt his heart pounding. It wasn't fair that someone like Carrie should have to live the way she did. There had to be something Scott could do to help her.

The question was, *what*?

Chapter Nine

The triplets were already at the G-Clef when Scott arrived. They'd been jamming on old Beatles tunes, waiting for their big brother.

"Nice of you to join us," Dave joked as he played the last chord of "Yesterday." "We've all been standing here wondering — where did Scott disappear to?"

"It was another great mystery — like who's selling Clint's old hair," Bob added.

The triplets started laughing hysterically. Scott stared at them. "Who's selling Clint's *what*?"

"Oh never mind," Dave replied. "You're really late. What are you on daylight saving time or something?"

"I knew you guys were going to get on my case. Actually I was having breakfast with a friend."

"Ooooo," Bob teased. "A friend? Leave it to

Scott to be here just one day and already have found a lady."

"Who said anything about my friend being a girl?"

The triplets laughed. "You don't usually blush when you talk about having breakfast with a guy, big bro," Clint deduced. "So give it up. What's her name?"

"Carrie."

"Is she coming to the concert? We want to meet her," Bob asked, speaking for the triplets.

"I don't think so," Scott replied sadly. "Her family's not from around here. They're sort of visiting Hollingsdale. And they probably have to be moving on."

"Sounds like us," Clint said.

"Not exactly," Scott replied somberly. "Carrie's family is homeless."

The triplets sat quietly as Scott explained how he had met Carrie. By the time Scott had finished telling them about his new friend's family, and how they'd lost everything, Bob, Clint, and Dave were on it — as determined as Scott to help the Parkers.

Suddenly, Bob got an idea. "You know, when we were up at the *Hollingsdale Times* offices, I was reading the paper while I was waiting to be photographed, and there was this article about an organization called Places for People. They find homes for families like Carrie's."

Clint's face lit up. "You mean they arrange for families to move into apartments in the area?"

Bob shook his head. "No. The article said that the people in the organization actually *build* the houses. You know, pour the cement, saw the wood, hammer the nails, and stuff like that. They get local architects and construction people to volunteer their time and expertise, and then other people just help out as best they can.

"After these families have a permanent place to live, it's much easier for them to get back on their feet. But I don't remember if the article actually mentioned *where* Places for People was building those homes. So even if Carrie and her family were eligible for one of the houses, they might have to move pretty far from here."

"I don't think they'd care," Scott told him. "From what Carrie was saying, her dad would go anywhere if he could find work."

"If you want, I can try to track down Places for People right after we rehearse," Bob offered. "The paper said they had offices in Hollingsdale. Maybe they really can help Carrie."

"That would be awesome." Scott thanked his brother. "In fact, do you think you could call now? I have an idea for a song, and I don't want to lose it."

"Go for it," Clint told Scott. "Dave and I can take a look at this sound system. They had some construction done recently, and the system got banged around a lot. Meanwhile you write your song, and Bob can make that call."

It was about three hours later when Scott finally picked his head up from his notebook. He'd been playing notes and chords the whole time. Finally, he walked over to where the triplets had been jamming without him.

"Any luck?" he asked Bob.

"I left a message with Places for People and told them they could call us here. How about you?"

Scott grinned. "I am officially unblocked. Listen to this."

Scott sat down on a stool in the middle of the stage. He picked up his guitar and strummed a sweet, wistful melody. Then he began to sing a song about a quiet girl who had been snatched away from everything she'd ever known, but had remained optimistic and hopeful for the future. It was possibly the most beautiful ballad Scott had ever written.

When he finished playing the final chord, Scott looked to his brothers for their opinion. The triplets stared at him in silence. To Scott, that meant more than applause. He had obviously touched an emotional chord with his brothers. They were speechless.

Finally, Dave broke the silence. "Amazing. Awesome. What do you call it?" he asked Scott.

"'Carrie.'"

Just then the phone rang. The manager of the G-Clef stepped out of the backstage office and peered out to the stage. "It's for you, Bob," he called out. "Someone from Places for People."

Bob ran to the office, his brothers following close behind. "Hi, this is Bob Moffatt," he said into the phone. "Yes, I called earlier about the girl and her family."

Scott was frustrated as he listened to Bob speak. He could only hear one side of the conversation. He had no idea what was going on.

"Oh, that would be amazing!" Scott heard Bob say. "Are you kidding? We'd love to. If that would help make sure they could get a house, count us in. No, I don't have to ask my brothers. They'd do it in an instant. We'll be there first thing in the morning. Oh! Thank you!"

As Bob hung up the phone, his brothers almost pounced on him.

"What did they say?" Dave asked.

"What don't you have to ask us?" Clint questioned his brother suspiciously. "Just what exactly have you gotten us into this time?"

Bob grinned. "How're you guys with a hammer and nails?" he asked mysteriously.

"I'm better with a guitar, but not too bad," Scott replied cautiously. "Why?"

"Well, it just so happens that Places for People is building a few homes right near here. Most of them have been assigned for months to families who need a fresh start. But one family just dropped out of the program because they were able to move in with a family member. Which leaves an empty, almost-finished house. The man on the phone told me Carrie's family could have that house — if *we* help build it. He figures the publicity of having the Moffatts working at the site would be great for their organization."

Scott was so excited he literally leaped into the air. "I've got to go tell Carrie!" he exclaimed. "She'll be so happy!"

As Scott dashed out of the arena, he practically ran over his father and Sheila as they walked in the artist's entrance.

"Where are you off to?" Frank asked Scott. "I thought you were rehearsing."

"Some things are too important to wait, Dad," Scott shouted as he ran past his dad and out onto the street.

"What was that all about?" Frank asked the triplets.

"Scott has some really good news for a girl," Clint explained.

"Does someone want to fill us in on what's been going on here?" Sheila asked.

Quickly, Bob told his parents all about Carrie and her family. Then he explained about the call he'd made to Places for People. "We have some free time tomorrow morning, anyway," he concluded. "This seemed like a good way to spend the time."

Frank took a deep breath as Bob finished talking. The look on his face told the guys that he wasn't quite as excited at the prospect of helping Carrie's family as they were.

"I'm awfully proud of you for wanting to help these people out of a jam," Frank began, choosing his words carefully. "And Places for People does sound like a wonderful cause to promote. But don't you think you should have asked Carrie's family if this was something they wanted, before you went ahead and committed them to living here in Hollingsdale?"

The triplets shook their heads. They'd been so caught up in coming to Carrie's rescue, they *had* forgotten to think about her feelings, or those of her parents and brother.

"I think maybe it's time I got involved," Frank told his sons. "Do any of you have an idea where Carrie and her family are now?"

"Scott said something about their van being parked outside an antique store that's a few blocks from the hotel, and around the corner from the coffee shop," Clint told his dad.

"Okay," Frank said. "I'll try there first. And cheer up, guys. It may just turn out that this is exactly what they were looking for. We just need to be sure."

Chapter Ten

Frank Moffatt reached the antique shop just in time to discover Scott standing outside the red van, trying to comfort Carrie. She was sobbing into a crumpled tissue. Her eyes were red, and her face was puffy. She'd obviously been crying for a while.

"I'm really sorry, Carrie," Scott told her. "We were just trying to help. I didn't think your dad would get upset. I figured he'd be happy that we'd come up with a solution to his problem."

Carrie wiped her eyes with a tissue. "I know you and your brothers were trying to help. And I'd really love to have a house again. But you have to understand that my dad's very proud. He doesn't want charity. He wants to be able to work for what he has. He's also really, really private. Being homeless is very embarrassing for him, so he especially didn't want me telling other people about our . . . uh . . . situation. I probably never should have talked to you about what happened to us. Dad's right. Some things are better kept to yourself."

Scott shook his head. "I respect your dad's feelings," he told Carrie. "But as for myself, if I keep problems bottled up inside, it drives me nuts. Everybody needs someone to talk to. I'm glad you picked me."

Frank walked over to Scott. "Hi, Scott. What's going on?" he asked.

"Dad!" Scott exclaimed with surprise. "What're you doing here?"

"Your brothers told me what's been going on. I wanted to talk to you about your idea."

"Yeah, well, you can forget about it now. Our plan didn't exactly work out the way we'd hoped." Scott stopped to introduce Carrie to his father. "Dad, this is Carrie Parker. Carrie, this is my dad, Frank Moffatt."

"Pleased to meet you, sir."

"It's a pleasure to meet you, Carrie," Frank replied. "My other sons filled me in on what Scott and his brothers wanted to do. I gather your family wasn't as excited as my boys were about Places for People's suggestion to help out."

"It's not that we weren't grateful, sir, it's just that . . . well . . . my dad really wants to make it on his own. He doesn't want someone to give us something for nothing."

Frank nodded understandingly. "I don't think that's how Places for People thinks of it. Your family will take part in building the house. And, once you're all on your feet, you'll be able to pay for some of it. Maybe even help others who are in a similar situation. I'd like to explain that to your dad. Do you think he'd talk to me?"

Carrie shrugged. "I don't know," she said. "He's pretty angry right now. He doesn't like that I told other people that he's out of work. But I'll ask him. At this point it can't do any harm to ask."

Carrie went into the van. It took a few minutes, but eventually she emerged, followed by a man in his early forties, dressed in a flannel shirt, jeans, and work boots. With his straight, blond, short hair, and deep-set green eyes, it was obvious that he was Carrie's dad.

"Hi, I'm Frank Moffatt," Scott's dad introduced himself, as he held out his hand.

"Chuck Parker," Carrie's dad replied, as he shook Frank's hand.

"I'm very pleased to meet you, Chuck," Frank said. "And I apologize for my boys' interference in your life. I assure you they didn't mean any harm. They were only trying to help a friend. Scott seems pretty fond of Carrie."

Scott and Carrie both blushed.

Chuck nodded at Frank, but he didn't say anything.

"I'd like to talk to you for a few minutes," Frank continued. "Would you like to go for a cup of coffee somewhere?"

Chuck looked at his daughter. Carrie's pleading eyes stared back at him.

"I suppose that would be all right," Chuck replied slowly. He turned to his daughter. "Carrie, tell your mom I'll be back soon. And then start working on those math problems she assigned you."

Frank turned to his son. "Scott, you'd better get back to the G-Clef," he told him. "There's another problem with the sound system, and I think you should get it worked out before you rehearse."

Carrie and Scott watched as their fathers walked down the street together.

"Do you think your dad can convince my dad to stay here in Hollingsdale?" Carrie asked.

"If anyone can do it, my dad can," Scott assured her.

After promising Carrie that no matter what her father decided he'd be sure to meet her at the coffee shop for lunch the next day, Scott walked to the arena and sat down on the stage. Dave, Clint, and Bob, who were all sitting at the sound board, walked over toward him.

"Did Dad find you?" Dave asked.

"Yeah, he found us, all right," Scott replied with a frown.

"I take it it didn't go so well with Carrie's folks," Clint remarked.

Scott shook his head. "I think her mom was probably okay with the idea of moving into a Places for People house, but her dad was really mad. He doesn't like to take help from people, I guess."

"He probably never played in a band then," Bob deduced. "We always have to depend on one another. Otherwise there'd be no harmonies."

Scott nodded. "Speaking of which, do you think you guys could put some harmonies to the melody line of my new song? And maybe give me some lyrics for the chorus? We may as well get some work done while we wait and see if Dad can convince Carrie's father to move into the Places for People house."

The Moffatts sat in a circle. Scott picked up his guitar, and began softly strumming while he sang his new song. One by one, his brothers joined in on the chorus, alternating singing high and low, until the sound was rich and smooth. As always, the guys' voices blended perfectly. Sometimes it seemed as though their four voices worked together to form a fifth, unique voice. It was a sound only brothers could achieve.

After working out the harmonies, they picked up their instruments, and prepared to rehearse "Raining in My Mind." They got about halfway through the song when the stage lights went out.

"Hey! What's going on?" Scott called out. "Who turned out the lights?"

Charlie, the manager of the G-Clef, dashed out of his office. "Sorry guys, we blew a fuse here. I'll have it fixed in a minute."

Dave sighed. "This venue is cool and all, but it sure could use someone good with his hands to keep it running."

The light flickered on and off for a second, and then came on permanently.

"Okay, guys, let's try it again," Bob ordered. He clicked his drumsticks together. "A five, six, seven, eight!"

And he launched into the song's first verse, one of Scott's favorites. It's about a boy who compares his girlfriend's sadness to storm clouds — and how he must wait for the sun to come out again.

As the guys started in on the song's second verse, Frank Moffatt walked into the arena. They stopped mid-song and jumped off the stage and ran toward their father.

"What did he say?" Scott spoke for all of them. "Are they staying in Hollingsdale?"

Frank sat down. "Well, I'm not sure. Carrie's dad is going to meet with the administrator of the local Places for People organization. He wants to be sure that he's able to give back to them. It turns out he's quite a capable guy. He worked in a factory in Brooklyn as the building superintendent. He can fix a lot of things."

"That's just what Carrie told me," Scott told his brothers.

"And speaking of fixing things," Frank continued, "I think that song you were just playing could use a little work. So you'd better get back to rehearsing. But just put in another hour or so, and then head back to the hotel. I want this to be an early night. Regardless of whether Carrie's family moves into that house, *you* four promised to help build it."

"Don't worry, Dad. We always keep our promises," Scott assured him. He had no doubt that he, Clint, Bob, and Dave would be at the Places for People building site early the next morning.

The question was, would Carrie's family be there to join them?

Chapter Eleven

Early the next morning the Moffatts hopped onto the tour bus and drove over to the Places for People building site. Although the guys and their parents had gotten to the site at the crack of dawn, plenty of volunteer workers had already arrived before them. The sounds of hammers and saws rang out as the bus pulled up.

As the Moffatts walked off the bus, a man in his mid-twenties, wearing a hard hat, jeans, work boots, and a Places for People T-shirt ran over to greet the boys.

"Hi, I'm Jeff Martin, publicity manager for Places for People," he introduced himself. "Boy, am I glad to see you. We're expecting quite a turnout today. Some of the photographers have already arrived, and there are a few TV crews who want to come out and interview you for the local morning shows. It's the most publicity we've gotten for the Hollingsdale project since it began!"

Scott looked out and quickly surveyed the crowd. He was hoping to see Carrie's dad among the workers who were busy putting the shingles on the roof of the house. But, unfortunately, he wasn't there.

Dave took one look at Scott's disappointed face, and put his arm around his brother's shoulder.

"Not here, huh?" he asked.

Scott shook his head. "I don't see the Parkers anywhere."

"Well, look, you tried to help her, okay? We *all* tried. There's nothing we can do about how her dad feels. And besides, we're here for a good cause, right?"

"Right!" Scott agreed, mustering as much enthusiasm as he could. He turned to Jeff. "So, where can a guy get a hammer around here?"

Jeff laughed. "Follow me, boys. I'll get you everything you need."

Scott was surprised at just how difficult construction work was. He and his brothers spent a good portion of the morning helping to put shutters on the second-story windows. It was a slow process. Everything had to be measured exactly, before eventually being hammered into place. The guys were especially conscious that each piece of wood had to be attached perfectly — and not just so the house would look good when a family moved in. As they climbed up on the ladders, and began hammering the shutters in place, the Moffatts had the added pressure of knowing that the press were taking photographs every step of the way. They didn't want to look lame in the next morning's paper.

As the guys hammered away, a group of fans gathered at the site. Eventually, Dave took a break from building, and walked over to talk to them.

"We'll be glad to sign autographs," Dave told the girls. "But there's a catch. You've got to pitch in and help. We want to get this house built quickly. The faster it goes up, the sooner a family without a home will have a place to live." As he spoke, Dave couldn't help but hope that somehow Carrie's father would change his mind and let the Parkers live in the house.

The fans got the message. Many of them went to work painting the doors of the house, while others set up the food carts, making sure everyone had enough to drink in the hot sun.

Clint went over to get a glass of lemonade. A tall, red-haired girl with big blue eyes handed him a cup. "Would you initial my locket?" she asked, pulling a black permanent marker from her pocket.

"Sure." Clint took the pen and reached over to write his initials on the hanging charm. But when he saw the charm up close, he stopped. It was the same charm the girls in the mall had been wearing. He opened the locket. Sure enough, there was a lock of dark-brown hair inside.

"Where did you get this?" he asked the fan.

"A man sold it to me yesterday, outside the record store on Green Street. He told me it was your hair. Don't you know him?"

Clint didn't answer her. He didn't want to upset the girl. She'd bought the locket in good faith. So, he just smiled, initialed the charm, and gave back her pen.

"Thanks for helping out," he said as he walked away.

Clint walked over to Bob. He was busy helping place shiny gold-colored doorknobs on the side door.

"That guy is still selling my hair — or at least what he *says* is my hair," Clint complained. "Some girl bought a locket with brown hair in it just yesterday."

"I wonder who it could be," Bob replied. "He's gotta stop pretty soon, when he runs out of hair."

"That's assuming that it really is my hair in there. I mean it looks like mine, but this guy could be using any brown hair."

By now, the sun was high in the sky, and Scott and the triplets were getting very tired. They'd already been working for three hours. Scott wiped a bead of sweat from his forehead, and hammered another nail into the shutters.

"I'll take over from here, Scott," a man's deep voice said from behind. Scott turned around slowly and came face-to-face with Chuck Parker.

"Mr. Parker!" Scott exclaimed. "I didn't think you . . . I wasn't sure . . . I . . . um . . ."

Chuck Parker laughed. "Carrie didn't mention anything to me about you having a tendency to get tongue-tied."

Scott blushed. "I don't usually. It sure is good to see you. Does this mean you're going to stay in Hollingsdale?"

"I have no choice," Chuck Parker replied. "I've got to be at work on Monday morning."

"Work?" Scott asked excitedly. "Really?"

"Yes. Your dad recommended I call that arena you boys are playing in tomorrow night. The place is really in need of repair. An outdoor stage takes a lot of beating from the weather, and the lighting needs to be adjusted continually. The manager agreed to hire me as the building superintendent. I'll fix what's broken, and then make sure that the G-Clef Arena stays in good shape all year 'round."

"That's so awesome!" Scott exclaimed.

"That's how I feel, too!" Chuck Parker chuckled. "It'll be awfully good to go back to work. I guess I learned something from you boys. It's not so bad to get a little help when you need it. I'll try and remember that the next time someone needs a bit of help from me."

Scott smiled broadly. It felt good to have helped to make such a major change in someone's life. And not just Mr. Parker's life, either. "Carrie must be *so* psyched," Scott exclaimed. "Now she'll be able to go back to school and everything." He looked around the construction site. "Where is Carrie? Is she here?"

Chuck Parker shook his head. "No. She mentioned something about having a lunch date at the coffee shop with a friend. Do *you* know anything about that?"

Scott looked at his watch. It was almost noon. He'd better hurry if he was going to meet Carrie for lunch.

"Since you're going to take over for me here, I think I'll go to lunch," Scott told Mr. Parker.

Chuck Parker grinned. "Have a good time. You deserve a break after all you and your brothers have done."

"Thanks!" Scott climbed carefully down the ladder and raced toward the coffee shop.

Chapter Twelve

Carrie was already waiting at the coffee shop when Scott arrived. She was sitting in the booth where she and Scott had had breakfast. It was hard to believe they'd only met a day ago. So much had changed in her life.

In just twenty-four short hours Scott could see a huge difference in the way Carrie looked. As he slid into the seat across from her he noted that her big green eyes were shining now, and she sat so much straighter, as though a huge weight had been lifted from her shoulders. To Scott, now Carrie really looked sixteen years old, instead of like an adult because she was carrying far too much responsibility.

"How are we ever going to thank you and your family?" Carrie asked Scott.

"Oh, you don't have to thank us," Scott insisted.

"But you've done so much for us. And there's nothing I can really do for you."

Scott thought about the beautiful new song he and his brothers were going to sing at their concert. It was sure to be a huge hit. Carrie'd been the inspiration that had freed him from writer's block. "Actually, you've already done a lot," he said mysteriously. "Much more than you know."

"I have? How?"

"If you come to the show tonight at the G-Clef, you'll see what I mean."

Carrie beamed. "I'll be there," she promised happily. "Did you know that my dad is going to be working there?"

Scott nodded. "He told me. But tonight he's not working. He's just going to kick back and enjoy himself. That's what I want all of you to do. I'll bet it's been a while since anyone in your family has been able to do that."

Carrie nodded silently.

"Great, then it's a done deal," Scott continued. "I'll leave a note at the door saying that you and your family are my guests. That way you'll get really good seats, right in front."

The waitress came by to take their order. Scott went for a burger, cheese fries, and a milk shake. Carrie just ordered a salad and a soda.

"Is that all you want?" Scott asked.

"I'm not so hungry anymore. I had a nice breakfast this morning."

"Where are you staying until the house is finished?" Scott asked Carrie.

"Places for People found us a room at a boardinghouse. It's nice there. We have our own bathroom and real mattresses. It's a little tight, I guess — but not compared to the van. And the boardinghouse isn't far from the school. Mom is taking Tom and me over on Monday to register. I know you love home-schooling, but I really missed being around other kids."

Scott looked at Carrie understandingly. "It's really different," he told her. "I mean, my brothers and I chose to go out on the road and pursue our dreams. You were forced into your situation. And it's a lot easier to study in a hotel room than in the back of a crowded van."

Carrie shrugged and looked down at the table. Scott could see that the memories were painful, so he hurried to change the subject.

"So tell me more about the boardinghouse," he suggested.

"Well, there are two other boarders. One's a woman who's about twenty-five. She just moved here, and she doesn't know anyone. She works at an insurance company. The other boarder is an old man we haven't met yet, but I hear all sorts of really cool jazz music coming from his room. The woman who owns the boardinghouse,

Mrs. Lamont, is really nice. She grew up in the house, and she raised her kids there, too. But they're all grown and have moved away. And her husband died a few years ago. But she's never alone, because she has a beautiful golden retriever named Lucky. She said my brother and I could play with him as long as we're living there. He's a really beautiful dog. I can't wait to move into our new house, but I think I'm gonna miss that dog a lot when we leave Mrs. Lamont's. We're buddies already." Carrie paused. "I'm going to miss you, too. I know you and your brothers are leaving Hollingsdale tomorrow."

Scott nodded. Then he smiled. "Well, we can keep in touch by mail. I don't really have a home address, like you're going to have. . . ." He stopped and laughed as Carrie grinned with excitement. "But I'll give you my manager's phone number and address. He'll get the mail to me. Or if your new school has computers, we can e-mail each other. So see, we'll stay friends forever."

Carrie blushed. "Great! It's just too bad Lucky doesn't know how to write letters."

Scott didn't say anything. He just smiled mysteriously to himself.

Chapter Thirteen

There was a big crowd already gathered outside the G-Clef as the Moffatts' tour bus pulled into the parking lot three hours before the show was scheduled to begin.

It seemed to Scott that fans were everywhere. There were at least 400 people — mostly teenage girls — hanging out on the street and in the parking lot. The kids were snacking on hero sandwiches and chips, and singing along to Moffatts songs that were blasting from portable stereos. A few of the teens had even brought along their own guitars and were playing some of the songs.

As soon as the fans spotted the bus, they stopped whatever they were doing and ran over to get a closer look at the Moffatts. Girls squealed with excitement as each brother got out of the bus and walked toward the door to the arena.

Although the arena entrance was only a few yards from the bus, it took the guys a while to reach the door. Kids were reaching out to them, trying to shake their hands, and asking for autographs. They didn't want to disappoint anyone. So even though they had a sound check to run before the show, they stood and talked to as many fans as possible, and autographed books, T-shirts, CDs, baseball hats, and even a pair or two of sneakers, before heading inside.

As Clint shook hands with a small brunette, he spotted a familiar face standing off to the side of the arena, a few yards from the throng of screaming girls. "You guys go ahead in," Clint told his brothers. "There's someone here I need to talk to."

As Bob, Dave, and Scott went inside, Clint walked over to the man. "Mr. Bratt," Clint called out. "I'm surprised to see you here. I thought you hated teenagers and pop stars."

The surly hotel manager gasped as he came face-to-face with Clint. Quickly, he closed a large suitcase that sat on the portable table in front of him.

"What's in there?" Clint asked.

"Nothing," Mr. Bratt muttered nervously. "Certainly nothing that you'd be concerned with."

"Are you sure?" Clint asked.

Before Mr. Bratt could respond, two girls

83

wearing Moffatts T-shirts walked over. "Clint! Could you sign our shirts?" they asked.

"Sure," Clint said.

One of the girls handed him her pen, and turned around so Clint could sign her back. Her friend did the same. Then they turned to Mr. Bratt. "Do you have any more of those lockets?"

Mr. Bratt gulped and kicked nervously at the ground. "What lockets?" he asked.

"You know, the ones with Clint's hair in them."

Clint shook his head with disgust. "I should have known it was you." He turned to the girls. "Of course he does, girls. They're right there, in his suitcase. Open it up and show them, Mr. Bratt."

Mr. Bratt looked curiously at Clint. "You mean you don't mind?" he asked.

"Mind?" Clint replied. "Why should I mind? Especially since you've promised to give *all* the proceeds from your sales to Places for People."

"I what?!" Mr. Bratt shouted.

"In fact, I'm going to make a big announcement about your generosity at the show tonight. By tomorrow, it'll be all over the press. You'll be a hero."

Mr. Bratt glared at Clint as he sold the girls their lockets. He'd never planned on giving cash to any charity. But now that he had been caught selling unauthorized Moffatts souvenirs — an act that was totally illegal — he had no choice. Better to give the money to Places for People than wind up in jail!

"See ya at the show, girls," Clint said as Mr. Bratt's customers walked off in the direction of the arena. When he was certain they were gone, he turned to Mr. Bratt. "What did you do — take the hair I'd left in the trash can in our suite bathroom?"

Mr. Bratt didn't say anything. He just stared suspiciously at Clint.

Clint flashed Mr. Bratt a triumphant smile and changed the subject. "Are you coming to the show tonight, Mr. B.?"

Mr. Bratt bristled at the nickname Clint had just given him. "I don't think so," he replied.

"Too bad. It's going to be quite a night!"

And as Clint walked off, Mr. Bratt muttered to himself, "I knew from the beginning those kids were going to be trouble!"

Chapter Fourteen

His brothers were already onstage running through their song list when Clint walked into the arena.

"What happened to you?" Bob asked him.

"We thought you'd been carried off by a group of beautiful girls," Dave added.

Clint laughed and shook his head. "Sorry. That's your dream, Dave."

"You know it!"

Clint picked up his bass and started tuning it. "Listen, I want to make a little announcement to the press tonight," he told his brothers as he tightened the pegs at the end of the bass.

"About what?" Scott asked.

"Let's just say I want to put a very hairy situation to rest — once and for all," Clint teased.

Scott shrugged. Sometimes his brothers seemed to be speaking a foreign language. This was one of those times.

After about an hour and half of running through the songs they would play that night, and putting the finishing touches on "Carrie," the Moffatts went backstage to put on their show clothes.

Clint pulled a perfectly pressed bright yellow suit from a dry-cleaning bag, and gently slipped on the pants, shirt, and jacket, trying his best not to wrinkle anything. Dave draped a lightweight leather jacket over his black shirt and checked himself out in the mirror. He knew that after a song or two he'd be very hot under the stage lights, and would slip the jacket off, but he figured it wouldn't hurt to look cool when he first came on the stage. As for Bob, he put on the new black-and-yellow surfer shirt he'd found at the Hollingsdale mall. It was light and roomy — perfect for jamming on the drums.

As Scott pulled a burgundy satin jacket over his black button-down shirt, he felt a little sad. This was their last night in Hollingsdale. After tonight, he probably would never see Carrie again. Even though they had promised to keep in touch, Scott knew they would probably not write to each other very often. Carrie would get involved in her new life, and he would move on with his career, and their letters would get further and further apart. That was just the way it was with pen pals. Still, Scott knew he would never forget Carrie. And he hoped that every time she turned on the radio and heard the song he'd written about her, Carrie would think of him, too.

Aruff! Just then, Harmony came bounding across the dressing room floor. He stopped at Bob's feet and waited patiently for the drummer to pet him.

"Where'd *he* come from?" Scott asked.

"I brought Harmony to see you guys," Frank Moffatt said as he walked into the dressing room. "I figured he might want to see one Moffatts show before the folks at the animal shelter got a chance to find him a new home."

Bob sighed. The thought of leaving the pup behind was very hard for him.

"I'm with you, Bob," Clint commiserated with his brother. "But let's not think about it now. It's only gonna bring us down. Listen to that crowd out there. Those people are totally psyched for the show! That should get you pumped!"

From their backstage dressing room, the Moffatts could hear the crowd beginning to file into their seats. The sound of fans laughing, calling out to one another, and even singing some Moffatts songs, was all the motivation the guys needed to get on stage. Already they could feel their adrenaline pumping — the way it always did when it was just a few minutes before show time.

Finally, the houselights went down. The owner

of the G-Clef took the stage. "Ladies and gentle-man," he shouted into the microphone. "Please give a huge Hollingsdale welcome to today's hottest rising pop stars. Ladies and gentlemen, I give you, THE MOFFATTS!"

The roar of the crowd was deafening as the boys took the stage.

Bob clicked his drumsticks together to start off the show. "Five, six, seven, eight," he shouted out. As he brought his stick down to meet the drum, his brothers started singing.

The song was one of the guys' favorites, about how hard it is for a boy to say those three little words, "I love you." It's also about his promise — if he ever *does,* it'll mean he's totally committed to her.

Scott smiled as he listened to the crowd singing along with "Say'n I Love You." He squinted in the light and looked down at the front row of seats. There, he found Carrie smil-ing up at him. She wasn't singing along, be-cause unlike the rest of the audience, she hadn't heard the song before. But Scott could tell she was enjoying the music. And from the looks of things, so were her parents and her brother, Tom. They were all nodding to the beat.

After a few seconds, Carrie realized Scott was looking at her. She blushed and waved. Scott winked at her.

As the song came to an end, the crowd cheered. Scott spoke into his microphone. "Hey there, Hollingsdale!" He punctuated his shout with a wild guitar riff and smiled as the audience exploded with applause. Bob picked up his sticks and started to beat out a drum solo.

Then Scott walked over to Clint's mike, "On keyboards, we've got the Wild Man, Mr. Dave . . . Moffatt!" Then he sauntered back to his own mike and shouted, "On the drums, we've got the Rhythm Meister himself, Mr. Bob . . . Moffatt!" After a brief pause, Scott continued, "And over here on bass, we've the Soul Man, my fellow Canadian, Mr. Clint . . . Moffatt!"

That was Clint's cue to step up to the mike and announce, "And over here on guitar, our older brother. We call him Elvis, Mr. Scott . . . Moffatt!"

The audience screamed and danced in their seats as the brothers put together an impromptu jam for a couple of minutes. When the music came to a stop, the crowd jumped to its feet and gave the guys a standing ovation.

"I hope this doesn't mean you're all ready to leave," Clint joked.

"No way!" the audience shouted back.

"Good! Because we have a whole night to party!"

The crowd cheered wildly.

Clint's expression changed slightly. "But I want to get serious here for just one minute," he said. "While we're partying, there are a lot of people out there with very little to be happy about. They're homeless. And they are a lot like you and me. But tonight, one man has agreed to help. Mr. Colin Bratt, the manager of our hotel, has been selling lockets with my hair in them to some of you. And I want you to know that just tonight, Mr. Bratt told me that all of the money he has raised will be donated to Places for People, so that some of those homeless families will soon have places to live!"

As the fans cheered, Scott, Dave, and Bob stared at Clint in disbelief.

"I should have known it was him. I just can't believe he planned to give all the money away for charity," Dave covered his microphone and murmured to Clint as the crowd continued to cheer.

"He didn't believe it, either — until I told him about it," Clint whispered back with a smile. "But now that I've announced it, he has no choice!"

Scott waited for the crowd to quiet down. "That's what life is all about — helping each other. Isn't it great that we can all be here for one another?" he asked the crowd. Then he and his brothers launched into "If Life Is So Short."

This song had special meaning for the guys. It was inspired just by a phrase people say all the time: "Life is short." In the Moffats' opening verse, a boy pleads to his crush to take a chance on love — since who knows what tomorrow will bring?

As the song moved into the chorus, Scott felt a few butterflies dancing around in the pit of his stomach. The next song on their set list was his new one, "Carrie." Scott was always a little worried about how a new song would go when it was performed live, and it was even more stressful to know that the girl who had inspired the song was sitting right there in the front row.

As soon as the guys sang their last notes of "If Life Is So Short," Scott smiled at Carrie. Then he looked out into the crowd and grinned.

"My brothers and I would like to thank you for being so kind to us while we were here in Hollingsdale. You are awesome!"

The crowd shouted back excitedly.

Scott waited for them to quiet down and then he continued. "We've met a lot of wonderful people, but I've made one special friend in particular. She's kind of new here herself, but I know you'll make her feel welcome. Carrie, this one's for you." He pointed his finger in Carrie's direction. She blushed and put her hands to her cheeks.

And with that, Scott strummed his guitar and began singing the soft, melodic song. As he and his brothers harmonized on the lyrics about a scared girl who has a lot on her mind, and even more in her heart, Scott tried not to look at Carrie. It would make singing the song even more difficult.

But Clint, Dave, and Bob weren't nearly as nervous. They watched as Carrie sat silent and still, smiling as the boys sang, and every now and then, wiping a tear from her cheek. At one point, her father put his arm around her shoulders, and gave Carrie a slight squeeze.

At the end, the audience went wild. They jumped to their feet and applauded like mad. If Scott had any doubts before, they were gone now. "Carrie" was a hit! Even more important, the song was a hit with Carrie. As soon as he'd finished singing, Scott had gathered enough courage to look at her. He found her standing on her chair, cheering with everyone else.

The Moffatts stayed late into the night, signing autographs and talking with their fans. As he signed copies of the group's CD, Scott scanned the crowd for Carrie. He wanted to tell her to meet him in the hotel lobby after the show. There was something he needed to ask her. But he couldn't find Carrie anywhere.

After the last fan had gone, the Moffatts

packed up their clothes and got back on their bus.

"We're leaving tomorrow, you know," Clint reminded the others as he scooped Harmony up in his arms.

"I know," Scott said sadly.

"Well, what are we going to do about this little chow hound?"

Bob sighed. "You know what we have to do. We have to give him to the shelter."

Scott shook his head. "Not necessarily. I have an idea — if it's okay with you guys."

As the bus rolled through Hollingsdale, Scott whispered something to the triplets.

"I've said it before and I'll say it again, big bro," Dave told Scott. "You definitely have random moments of genius."

When the guys got back to the hotel, it was after eleven. The lobby was empty, except for the two young clerks who were working the desk. But as Scott walked toward the elevator, he noticed someone sitting on a couch in the corner, fast asleep.

"Go on up," Scott told his brothers as he walked toward the couch. "I'll be there in a minute."

As the elevator door closed behind his brothers, Scott sat down on the couch next to Carrie and gently tapped her on the shoulder.

"Hey sleepyhead. Wake up," he whispered gently.

Carrie's eyes fluttered open slowly. She pushed a lock of blond hair from her face, looked at Scott, and smiled. "What time is it?" she asked.

"About eleven."

"Uh-oh," she groaned. "My dad dropped me off here after the show. He's coming back to pick me up at eleven-thirty. That doesn't give me much time. I just wanted to thank you — for the tickets, for the song, for everything. I know you're leaving early, so . . ."

Scott stopped her. "Listen, I need you to do me a favor."

"Anything."

"I know someone who needs a home really badly. And I think your family might be able to give it to him."

Carrie looked confused. "We can?"

Scott nodded. "His name is Harmony, and he's a little weird-looking, but kind of cute when you get used to him."

Carrie wrinkled her forehead, confused.

Scott grinned. "Oh, did I mention that he's a dog?"

Carrie squealed with delight. "A dog! Oh, Scott, this is the best . . ."

"Whoa! Wait a minute," Scott cautioned. "I think you'd better ask your parents if you can keep him — especially after what happened the last time. If they say it's okay, then meet my family here at the hotel at about nine tomorrow morning."

"I'll be here," Carrie assured Scott. "My folks will say yes. I know they will."

Chapter Fifteen

The next morning, the Moffatts put their clothes back into suitcases and traveling bags and loaded them onto the tour bus. On his way out of the hotel, Clint stopped off at the front desk. He slapped a copy of the morning paper on the counter.

"Did you check out page six, Mr. B.?" Clint asked Mr. Bratt. "It's a review of our show last night. They liked it a lot. But they were especially impressed with *your* generosity."

Mr. Bratt didn't answer Clint. He just snarled and glanced down at the story on page six of the *Hollingsdale Times*. Sure enough, the caption beneath Clint's picture read, "Clint Moffatt announces a generous donation to Places for People from Hollingsdale's own Colin Bratt. The funds came from sales of Moffatts merchandise."

Clint smiled as he watched Mr. Bratt read the newspaper. "A Places for People representative will be here at two o'clock to collect the check. I think the *Hollingsdale Times* is sending a photographer to record the moment. Congratulations! You're a local celebrity."

Mr. Bratt sighed. There was no getting out of this one.

"See ya around Mr. B.!" Clint called back to the desk as he left the hotel for the last time.

Most of the equipment had been packed onto the bus the night before, but Scott made sure to bring his guitar on board. Scott was very attached to his guitar, and rarely let it out of his sight. Besides, he never knew when an idea for a new song would come to him. Since writing "Carrie," Scott had sketched out at least five new melodies. He hoped he and his brothers could work together to flesh them out into songs.

As Scott was leaving the hotel, he put Harmony under his jacket. He didn't want any last-minute hassles from Mr. Bratt. But as soon as he got outside, he put the dog down, and looked around. There was no sign of Carrie.

"It doesn't look like Carrie's parents gave her the okay, son," Frank said softly, placing a compassionate hand on his son's shoulder. "I think we're going to have to take Harmony to the shelter. But don't worry — they'll find him a good home. I'm sure of it."

"Can't we wait just five more minutes?"

Frank shook his head. "We're already almost fifteen minutes behind schedule. We have to face facts. Carrie's not coming. Come on. Put Harmony on the bus, and we'll drive over to the shelter."

Scott did as he was told. He lifted the dog in his arms and slowly boarded the bus. The driver closed the door behind him, and turned on the engine. But just as the bus began to move through the parking lot, Scott heard a horn honking. He looked out the window to see an old red van driving up beside them.

Carrie stuck her head out from the passenger side window. "Scott! Wait!" she cried out as loudly as she could. "They said yes! My parents said yes!"

"STOP THE BUS!" Scott called to the driver. "Carrie's here."

The bus screeched to a halt. Scott scooped Harmony up in his arms and ran to the front. The triplets followed close behind.

"I'm so sorry we're late," Carrie apologized. "We had to wait for Mrs. Lamont to wake up so we could ask if Harmony could stay at the boardinghouse with us until our house was ready. I was afraid we'd missed you."

"You almost did," Scott told her. "But you got here just in time."

Carrie reached out to pet the little dog gently along his back. "Is this Harmony?" she asked.

Scott nodded.

"I can't believe you said he was weird-looking. I think he's adorable," Carrie playfully scolded Scott.

"To each his own," Bob muttered.

"Can I hold him?" Carrie asked.

Scott looked down at Harmony. He knew this was good-bye. "Of course you can," he told Carrie softly. "He's yours now."

Carrie took Harmony in her arms. At first, the pup stiffened. He was afraid. But Carrie's gentle petting soon calmed his fears, and he seemed to relax a bit.

"We'll take him down to the animal shelter to have him checked out, and to give him his shots," Carrie said. "He'll have the best of care — and lots of love. I promise you guys that."

"We know he will," Clint replied. "Thanks for taking him."

"Thank *you*! Thank you for everything!" Carrie told him, adding that her dad was really looking forward to his new job at the G-Clef arena the next day.

"Boys, we've got to get moving!" Frank called from the bus window.

The Moffatts nodded.

"Well, I guess this is good-bye," Carrie said as Scott turned toward the bus.

"Maybe we'll be back here again," Scott suggested.

"I hope so," Carrie answered. "Harmony and I would like that." She gave Scott a small peck on the cheek, and then blushed beet-red. "Take care."

"You, too," Scott told her. Then he boarded the bus.

An hour later, as the bus headed out of New York and into Pennsylvania, Scott sat on his bunk and began to sketch out a new melody. A soft spongy football soared across the bus and bonked him right on the head.

"Oops!" Dave said as he walked over and picked up the ball. "Sorry. We were just having a catch. I guess I forgot we were back in tight quarters again."

Scott just smiled and tossed the ball across the aisle toward Clint, joining in on the fun. For the time being at least, the tour bus was the Moffatts' home. And deep in his heart, he knew that he would never complain about it again. Life on the road had its ups and downs, just like everything else. But the Moffatts were a very lucky family. At the moment, however, there *was* one little thing bothering Scott.

As the bus rolled past a sign advertising a rest stop, Scott felt that old familiar rumbling in his stomach. "Hey dad!" he called out. "What do you say we stop for lunch?"

CALLING ALL MOFFATTS MANIACS!

ENTER NOW AND YOU MIGHT BE THE LUCKY WINNER OF THE MOFFATTS CONCERT SWEEPSTAKES!

Scholastic will fly four people (you, for example, with two friends and a guardian) to a yet-to-be-determined location to see The Moffatts in concert! Plus, you and your crew will be taken backstage for a party where you will personally meet all of The Moffatts!

All you have to do is fill out the form below and send it in to:
THE MOFFATTS CONCERT Sweepstakes, c/o Scholastic Inc.,
P.O. Box 7500, Jefferson City, MO 65101 by October 15, 2000.

Here's your chance to go from "MISERY" to "MANIA!"

Official Rules:

1. NO PURCHASE NECESSARY. To enter, complete this official entry coupon or hand print your name, address, birthdate, and telephone number on a 3" x 5" card and mail to: THE MOFFATTS CONCERT Sweepstakes, c/o Scholastic Inc., P.O. Box 7500, Jefferson City, MO 65101. Entries must be postmarked by 7/1/00. Scholastic is not responsible for late, lost, stolen, damaged, misdirected, or postage due entries.

2. Sweepstakes open to residents of the USA no older than 16 as of 12/1/00, except employees of Scholastic Inc., and Capitol Records their respective affiliates, subsidiaries, and their respective advertising, promotion, and fulfillment agencies, and the immediate families of each. Sweepstakes is void where prohibited by law.

3. Winners will be selected at random on or about 7/05/00, by Scholastic Inc., whose decision is final. Odds of winning are dependent on the number of entries received. Except where prohibited, by accepting the prize, winner consents to the use of his/her name, age, entry, and/or likeness by sponsors for publicity purposes without further notice or compensation. Winners will be notified by mail and will be required to sign and return an affidavit of eligibility and liability release within fourteen days of notification, or the prize will be forfeited and awarded to an alternate winner.

4. Grand Prize: A two (2) day, one (1) night trip for four people (includes winner, two friends, and one guardian), plus four performance tickets, to see The Moffatts in concert (date and exact location of trip to be determined by sponsor on or about July 15, 2000). Includes round-trip coach, air transportation from airport nearest winner's home to the destination, one night's lodging and meals. Travel must include Saturday night stay. (Est. retail value of prize $2,500)

5. Prize is non-transferable, not returnable, and cannot be sold or redeemed for cash. No substitutions allowed, unless by Scholastic due to unavailability. All taxes on prize, if any, are the sole responsibility of the winner. By accepting the prize, winner agrees that Scholastic Inc. and Capitol Records their respective officers, directors, agents, and employees will have no liability or responsibility for injuries, losses or damages of any kind resulting from the acceptance, possession, or use of any prize and they will be held harmless against any claims of liability arising directly or indirectly from the prizes awarded.

6. For a list of winners, send a self-addressed stamped envelope after 7/15/00 to THE MOFFATTS CONCERT Winners, c/o Scholastic Inc., Trade Marketing Dept., 555 Broadway, New York, NY, 10012.

YES! Enter me in THE MOFFATTS CONCERT Sweepstakes.

Name_____ Birthdate_____

Address_____

City_____ State_____ Zip_____

MOF600